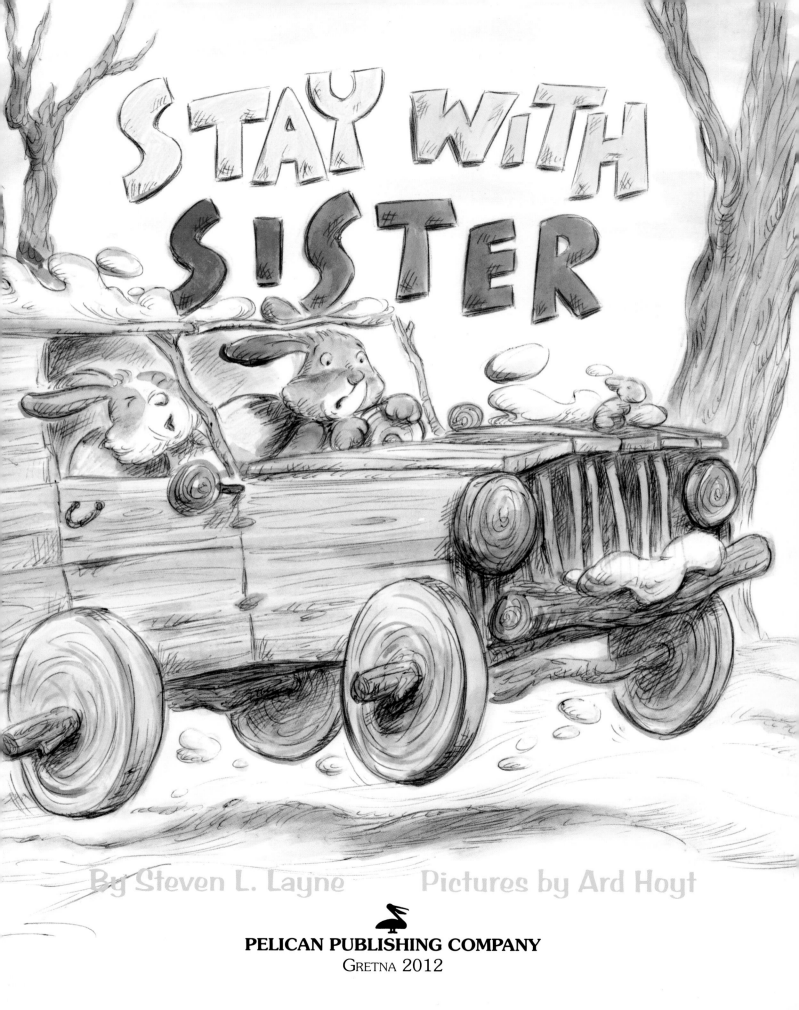

STAY WITH SISTER

By Steven L. Layne   Pictures by Ard Hoyt

PELICAN PUBLISHING COMPANY

GRETNA 2012

To "Aunt" Esther Hershenhorn, who helps every manuscript that
crosses her path to be more than it might ever have been—SL

*The word "Pelican" and the depiction of a pelican are
trademarks of Pelican Publishing Company, Inc., and are
registered in the U.S. Patent and Trademark Office.*

ISBN: 9781455615230
E-book ISBN: 9781455615247

Printed in Singapore
Published by Pelican Publishing Company, Inc.
1000 Burmaster Street, Gretna, Louisiana 70053

I was writing a note to Santa the day Mommy and Daddy brought Sister home. Brother was only a little excited. I was very excited. I knew all about babies. I was going to be a lot of help!

Being a lot of help is fun sometimes . . .
but not all the time.

Sister causes problems.

And now that she's a little older, the problems are even worse.

Sister talks all the time, and she plays with boring toys. Sometimes, she does things that Mommy and Daddy don't like. And she's always making big messes that she can't clean up by herself.

Sister especially likes to wander off, so she
needs someone watching her every minute . . .

and sometimes that someone is me!

Last Halloween, Mommy took us to Cackles and Grins. Brother wanted to walk through Haunted Turnip Tower.

"Stay with Sister. She might feel scared," Mommy told me.

I held Sister's hand until a spook jumped
out at me.

Sometimes Mommy can be scarier than a spook. She found Sister playing in an ugly witch's brew.

Sister didn't look very scared to me.

Every year, Nana shops for a new Easter bonnet. Last spring, she took us with her because we promised to be good.

Brother and I know all about staying close. Sister likes exploring though, so Nana put me in charge.

"Stay with Sister. She might get lost," Nana said.

We decided playing a game with Sister would be fun, so Brother and I picked hide-and-go-seek. Nana didn't think we made a very good choice.

She found Sister sitting on the Easter Bunny's lap.
Sister didn't look very lost to me.

It didn't matter where I went.
Someone was always telling me,

"Stay with Sister!"

The nurse in Dr. Towner's office said it
in the waiting room. Our neighbor Mrs.
Wilson said it on the trip downtown.
But then, when my Aunt Esther said it
at the village fireworks,

I made my angry face
and threw my
sparklers on the ground.

Today, Daddy took Brother and me swimming. Sister came too, but she had to play on Celery Island because she can't swim.

When Daddy went to order lunch, he sent *me* to Celery Island!

"Stay with Sister. She might get hurt,"

Daddy hollered.

Sister cried when I started a splash contest, so I went sailing in Radish Rapids.

"Somebody else can stay with Sister!"
I shouted.

And somebody else did.

Daddy found her playing at the lifeguard station. He was not happy at all.

Sister didn't look very hurt to me, and this time I said so!

When we got home, Daddy sent me to my room.

After dinner, I heard Brother watching *Blastoff Bunny* without me, and I felt very sad. Sister tippy-toed in. I pretended she wasn't there. She said we could wear dress-up clothes. I said,

"I don't wear pink."

She asked me to a tea party. I shook my head,

"I'm full."

She offered me her favorite dolls. I laughed and said,

"They're girl toys."

When she tried to read my favorite book,
my insides felt all funny.

Sister waved goodbye, but I wanted her to stay.

"Stay with brother?"

I asked.

Sister smiled.

"Okay."

And you know what?
As long as no one sees us . . .
that's okay with me.